DINOPEDIA

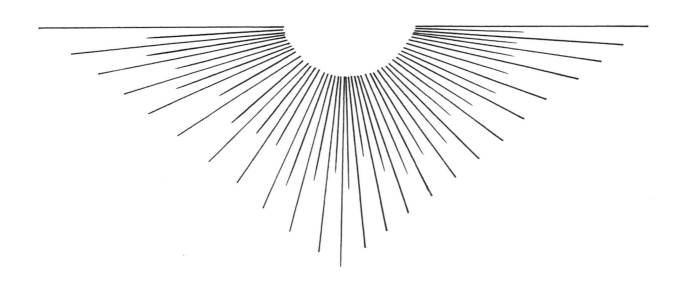

LAURENCE KING

First published in the United States in 2024 by
Laurence King

HB ISBN: 9781510230668

10 9 8 7 6 5 4 3 2 1

Printed in China

FSC
www.fsc.org
MIX
Paper | Supporting
responsible forestry
FSC® C104740

Laurence King
An imprint of
Hachette Children's Group
Part of Hodder and Stoughton
Carmelite House
50 Victoria Embankment
London EC4Y 0DZ

An Hachette UK Company
www.hachette.co.uk
www.hachettechildrens.co.uk
www.laurenceking.com

DINOPEDIA

AN ENCYCLOPEDIA OF
PREHISTORIC BEASTS

Tom Jackson

Good Wives and Warriors

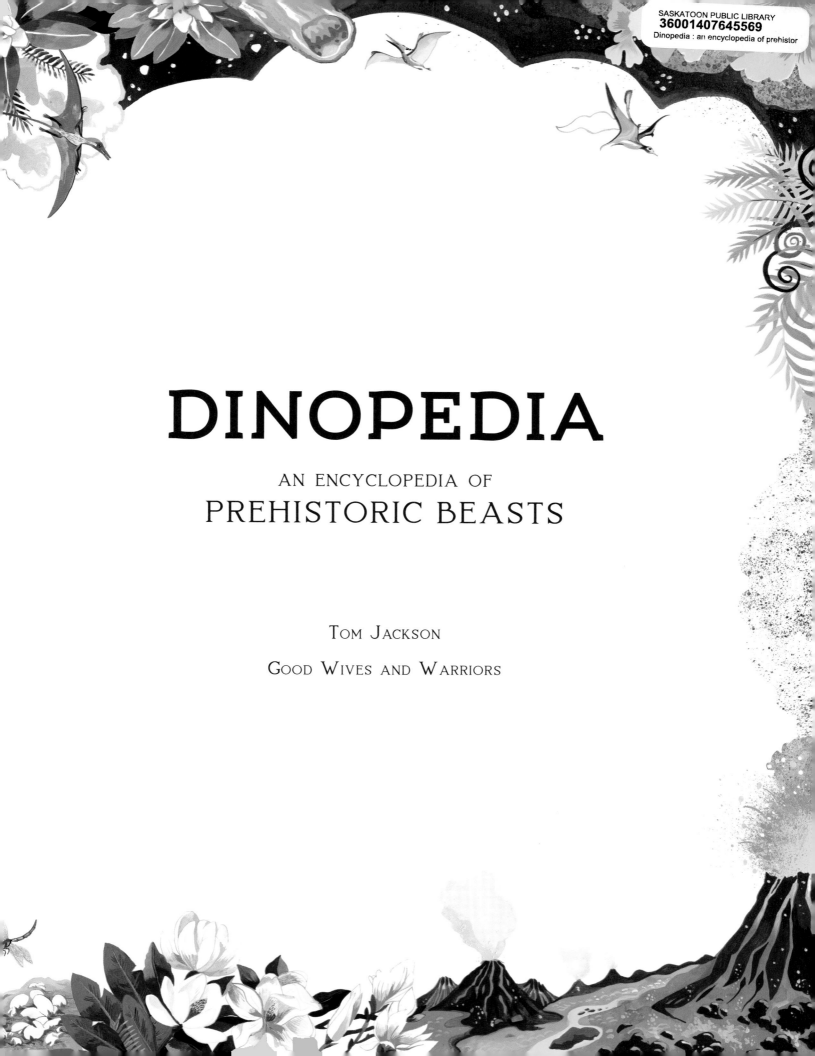

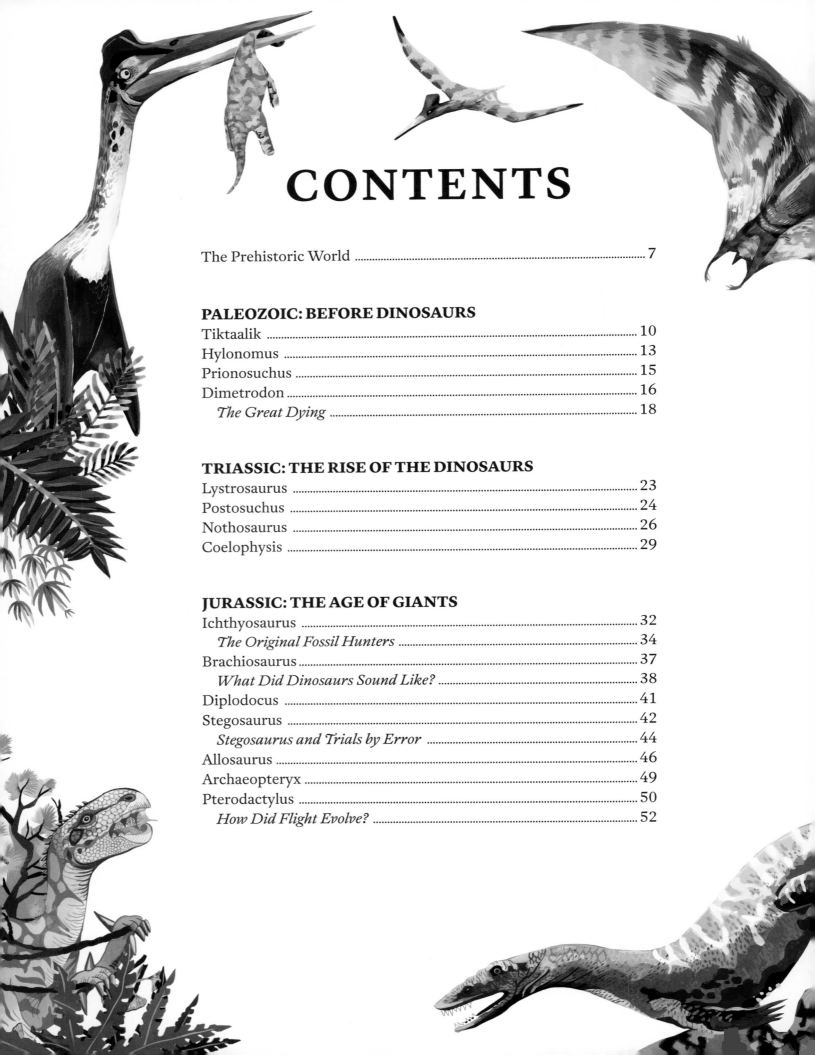

CONTENTS

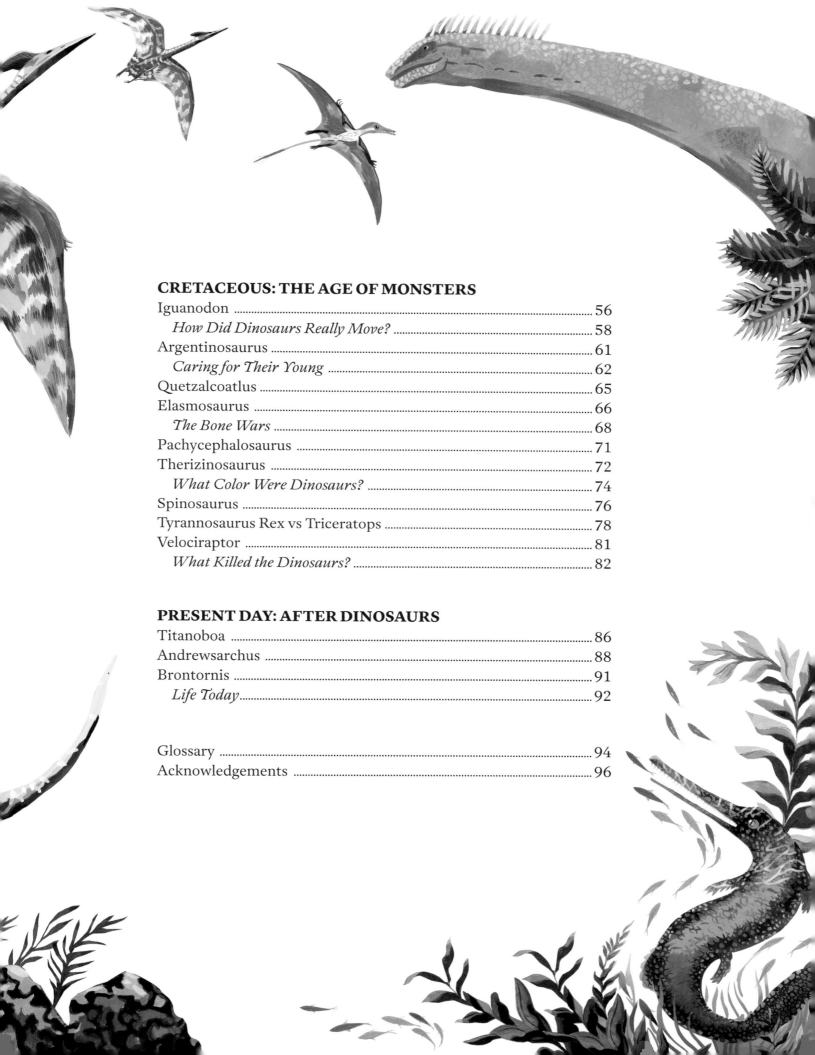

CRETACEOUS: THE AGE OF MONSTERS

PRESENT DAY: AFTER DINOSAURS

THE PREHISTORIC WORLD

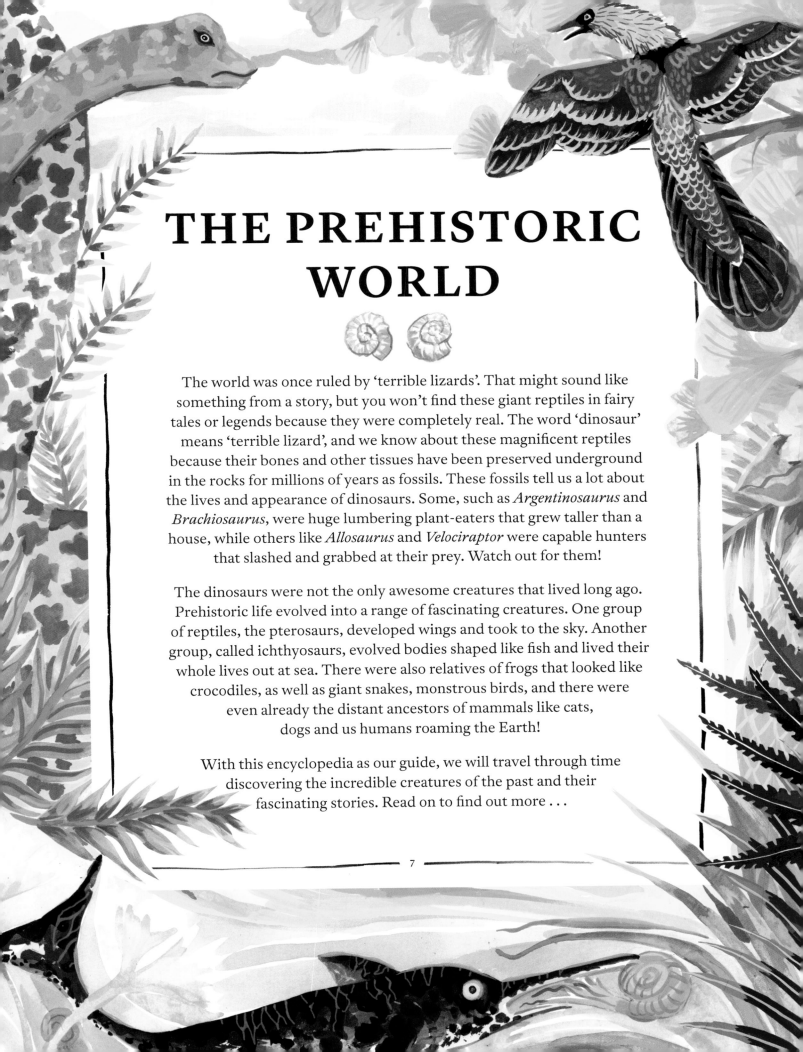

The world was once ruled by 'terrible lizards'. That might sound like something from a story, but you won't find these giant reptiles in fairy tales or legends because they were completely real. The word 'dinosaur' means 'terrible lizard', and we know about these magnificent reptiles because their bones and other tissues have been preserved underground in the rocks for millions of years as fossils. These fossils tell us a lot about the lives and appearance of dinosaurs. Some, such as *Argentinosaurus* and *Brachiosaurus*, were huge lumbering plant-eaters that grew taller than a house, while others like *Allosaurus* and *Velociraptor* were capable hunters that slashed and grabbed at their prey. Watch out for them!

The dinosaurs were not the only awesome creatures that lived long ago. Prehistoric life evolved into a range of fascinating creatures. One group of reptiles, the pterosaurs, developed wings and took to the sky. Another group, called ichthyosaurs, evolved bodies shaped like fish and lived their whole lives out at sea. There were also relatives of frogs that looked like crocodiles, as well as giant snakes, monstrous birds, and there were even already the distant ancestors of mammals like cats, dogs and us humans roaming the Earth!

With this encyclopedia as our guide, we will travel through time discovering the incredible creatures of the past and their fascinating stories. Read on to find out more . . .

PANGAEA

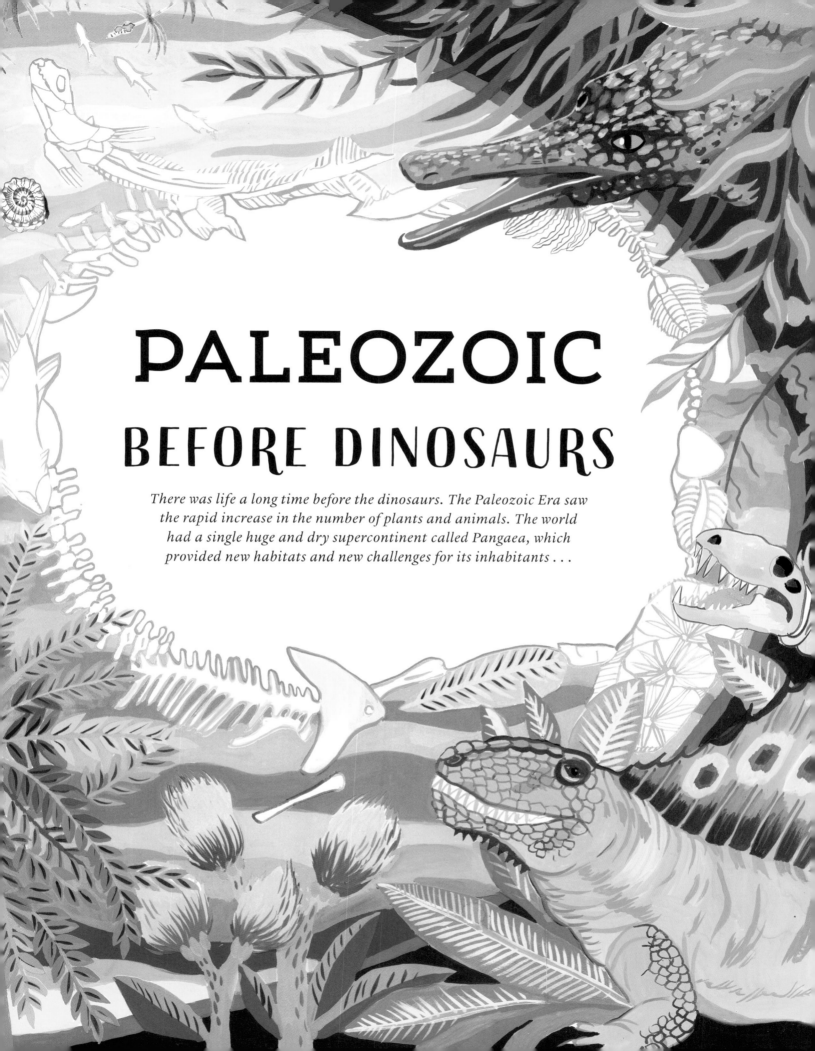

PALEOZOIC

BEFORE DINOSAURS

There was life a long time before the dinosaurs. The Paleozoic Era saw the rapid increase in the number of plants and animals. The world had a single huge and dry supercontinent called Pangaea, which provided new habitats and new challenges for its inhabitants . . .

of so many animals. Vast quantities of greenhouse gases like carbon dioxide and methane were released into the atmosphere and that quickly changed the climate, making the world warmer. Marine organisms struggled to handle these new temperatures, and the warmer waters decreased the amount of oxygen available while also becoming more acidic. Eruptions also release various metals, which can poison marine environments, therefore making the animals in the seas very sick.

Methane gas bubbling into the air

On land, the effects of the eruptions may have lasted for around a million years. Increased drought and wildfires turned parts of the land to ashes and animals tried to migrate away from the scorching equator. The gases released by the eruptions also affected the atmosphere and ozone layer. Some gases mixed with water to produce acid rain, which is very harmful to the environment, while others reduced the protective function of the ozone layer, allowing more harmful radiation from the sun to seep through. This caused plants to produce fewer offspring, meaning there was less food available for plant-eaters.

However, life on Earth did not end. It took around 10 million years for life to recover and form stable ecosystems in the Triassic, but some of the most remarkable creatures evolved in this new world. One very important group were the archosaurs, a group of reptiles that includes some of the most successful land animals to have ever lived: the dinosaurs.

Archosaurus

LAURASIA

GONDWANA

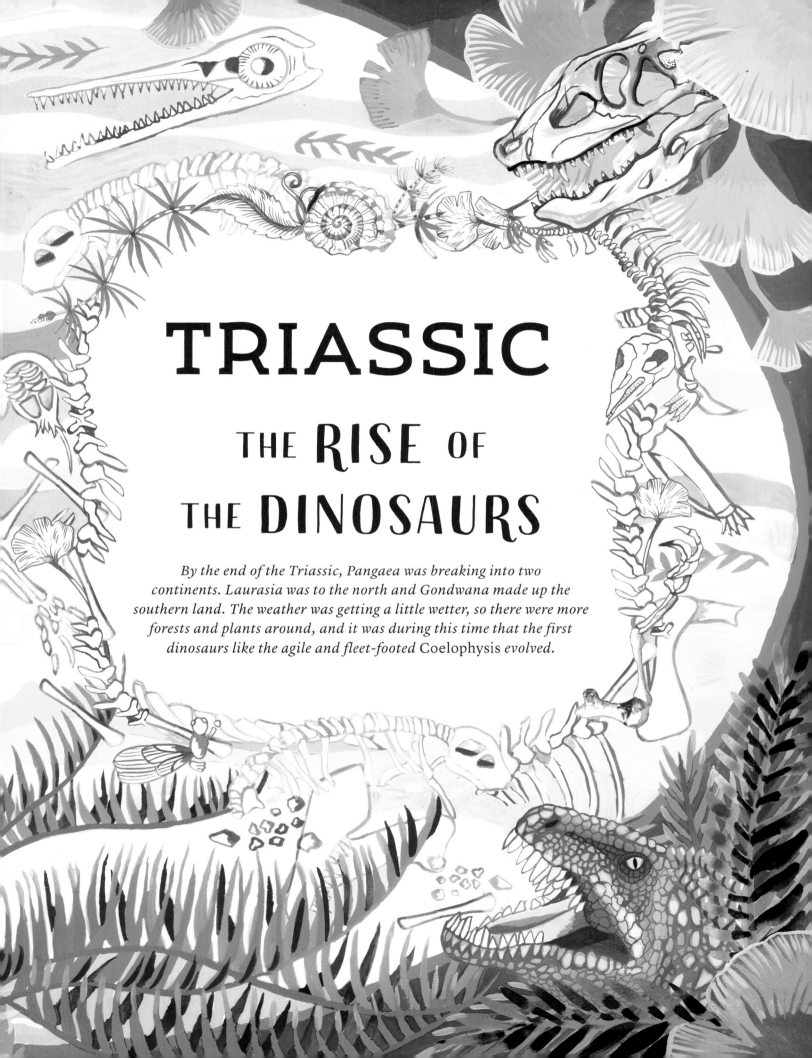

TRIASSIC

THE RISE OF THE DINOSAURS

By the end of the Triassic, Pangaea was breaking into two continents. Laurasia was to the north and Gondwana made up the southern land. The weather was getting a little wetter, so there were more forests and plants around, and it was during this time that the first dinosaurs like the agile and fleet-footed Coelophysis evolved.

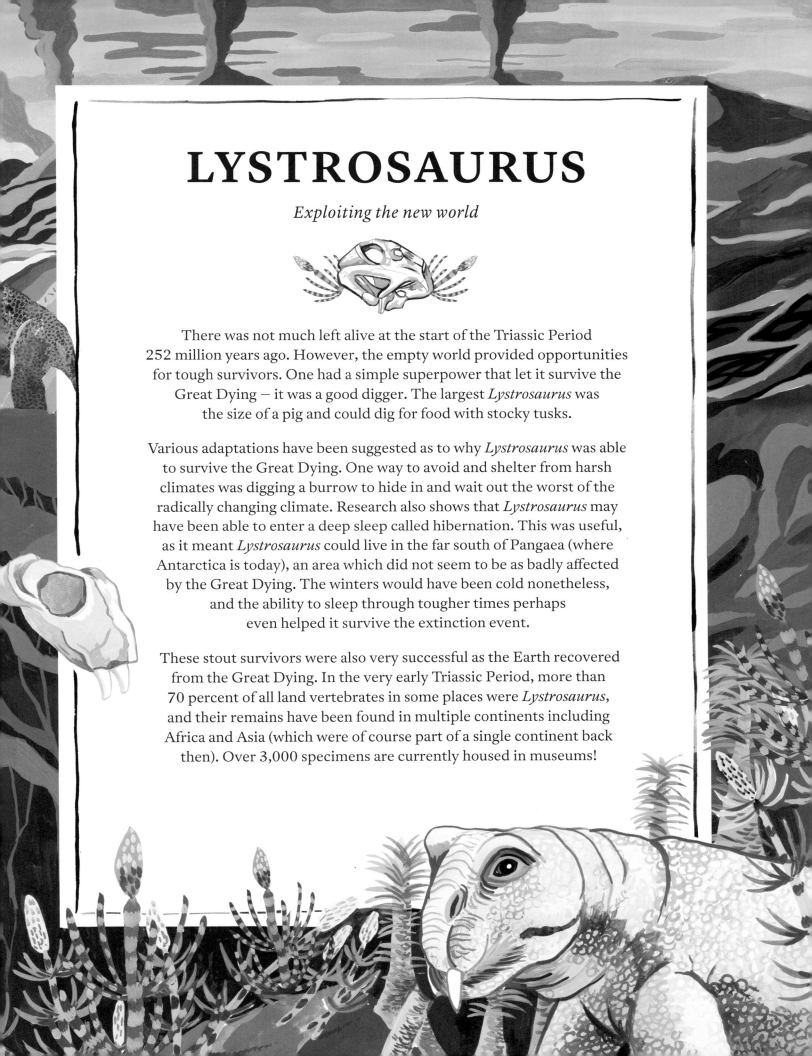

LYSTROSAURUS

Exploiting the new world

There was not much left alive at the start of the Triassic Period 252 million years ago. However, the empty world provided opportunities for tough survivors. One had a simple superpower that let it survive the Great Dying – it was a good digger. The largest *Lystrosaurus* was the size of a pig and could dig for food with stocky tusks.

Various adaptations have been suggested as to why *Lystrosaurus* was able to survive the Great Dying. One way to avoid and shelter from harsh climates was digging a burrow to hide in and wait out the worst of the radically changing climate. Research also shows that *Lystrosaurus* may have been able to enter a deep sleep called hibernation. This was useful, as it meant *Lystrosaurus* could live in the far south of Pangaea (where Antarctica is today), an area which did not seem to be as badly affected by the Great Dying. The winters would have been cold nonetheless, and the ability to sleep through tougher times perhaps even helped it survive the extinction event.

These stout survivors were also very successful as the Earth recovered from the Great Dying. In the very early Triassic Period, more than 70 percent of all land vertebrates in some places were *Lystrosaurus*, and their remains have been found in multiple continents including Africa and Asia (which were of course part of a single continent back then). Over 3,000 specimens are currently housed in museums!

In crocodilians, this structure helps make deep bellowing calls to attract mates as well as communicate with offspring. Amazingly, the larynx of one dinosaur, an armored herbivore called *Pinacosaurus*, is known. Based on its structure, the larynx could possibly open its airway wide to make loud calls. The windpipe could also change shape to make other noises. Additional finds are needed in order to better understand the function of the larynx in *Pinacosaurus*, and what it means for dinosaur noises.

By analyzing the shape of the inner ear in fossil skulls, it seems that many sounds made by large dinosaurs were probably low-pitched as well. The cochlea, a part of the inner ear involved in hearing, is relatively long in many dinosaurs, suggesting they could pick up low noises well. And some of the noisiest dinosaurs were probably the hadrosaurs. These big plant-eaters had complex social lives, and many developed bony, hollow crests. *Parasaurolophus* had a 6.5 ft crest with a looping tube inside. It is suggested that *Parasaurolophus* used this feature to help communicate with others.

Experts aren't certain about what dinosaurs sounded like, but the loudest bird and reptile calls today are deep booms and whoops. If we could go back in time to the mighty days of the dinosaurs, perhaps we'd hear those sounds fill the air even then.

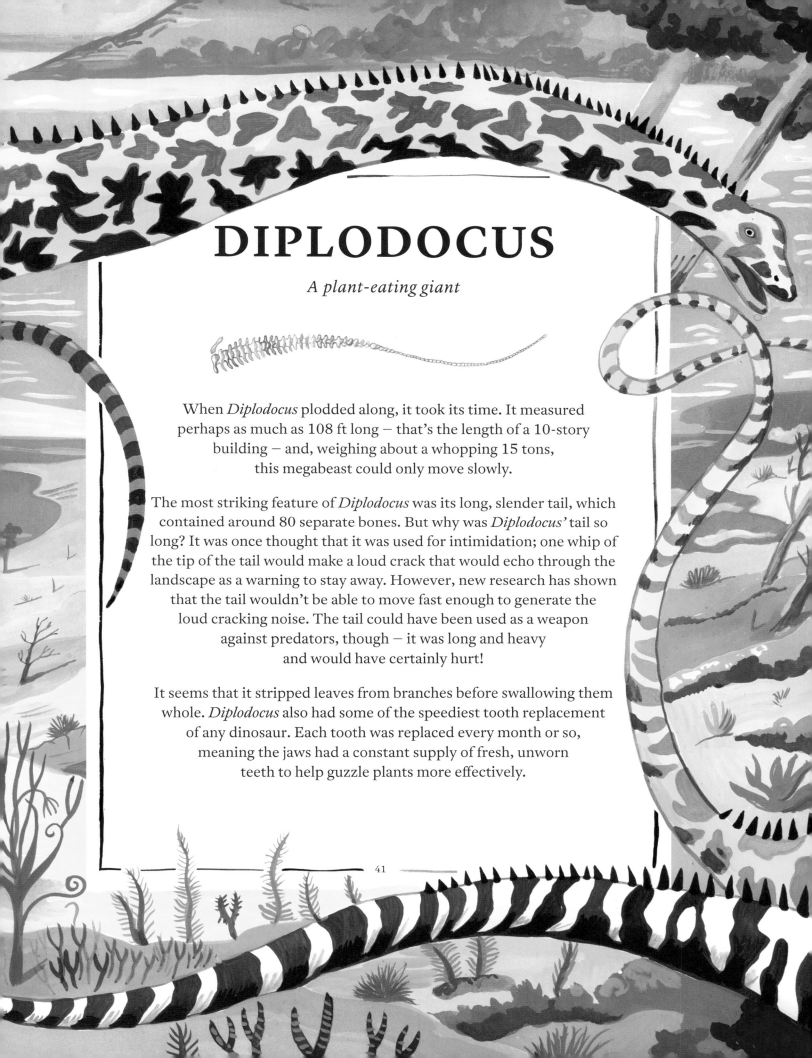

DIPLODOCUS

A plant-eating giant

When *Diplodocus* plodded along, it took its time. It measured perhaps as much as 108 ft long – that's the length of a 10-story building – and, weighing about a whopping 15 tons, this megabeast could only move slowly.

The most striking feature of *Diplodocus* was its long, slender tail, which contained around 80 separate bones. But why was *Diplodocus'* tail so long? It was once thought that it was used for intimidation; one whip of the tip of the tail would make a loud crack that would echo through the landscape as a warning to stay away. However, new research has shown that the tail wouldn't be able to move fast enough to generate the loud cracking noise. The tail could have been used as a weapon against predators, though – it was long and heavy and would have certainly hurt!

It seems that it stripped leaves from branches before swallowing them whole. *Diplodocus* also had some of the speediest tooth replacement of any dinosaur. Each tooth was replaced every month or so, meaning the jaws had a constant supply of fresh, unworn teeth to help guzzle plants more effectively.

41

STEGOSAURUS

An armored giant

Around 150 million years ago the *Stegosaurus* could be seen lumbering through the open countryside of what is now North America and Europe. The *Stegosaurus'* brain was only the size of a small fruit, controlling a body that was up to 29.5 ft long from nose to tail tip. That is the length of a school bus — so you can imagine how heavy it was too!

Stegosaurus was an unsual stegosaur, with large plates on its back rather than the more typical spikes seen in many of its relatives. These probably played a role in display, while the spiked tail was used to defend against predators.

The small, narrow skull was useful for eating low-lying plants. It had a stronger bite compared to dinosaurs with similar skull shapes, and probably ate tough plants. Its huge gut helped digest its meal, and it spent much of its day eating and eating — and then eating some more.

42

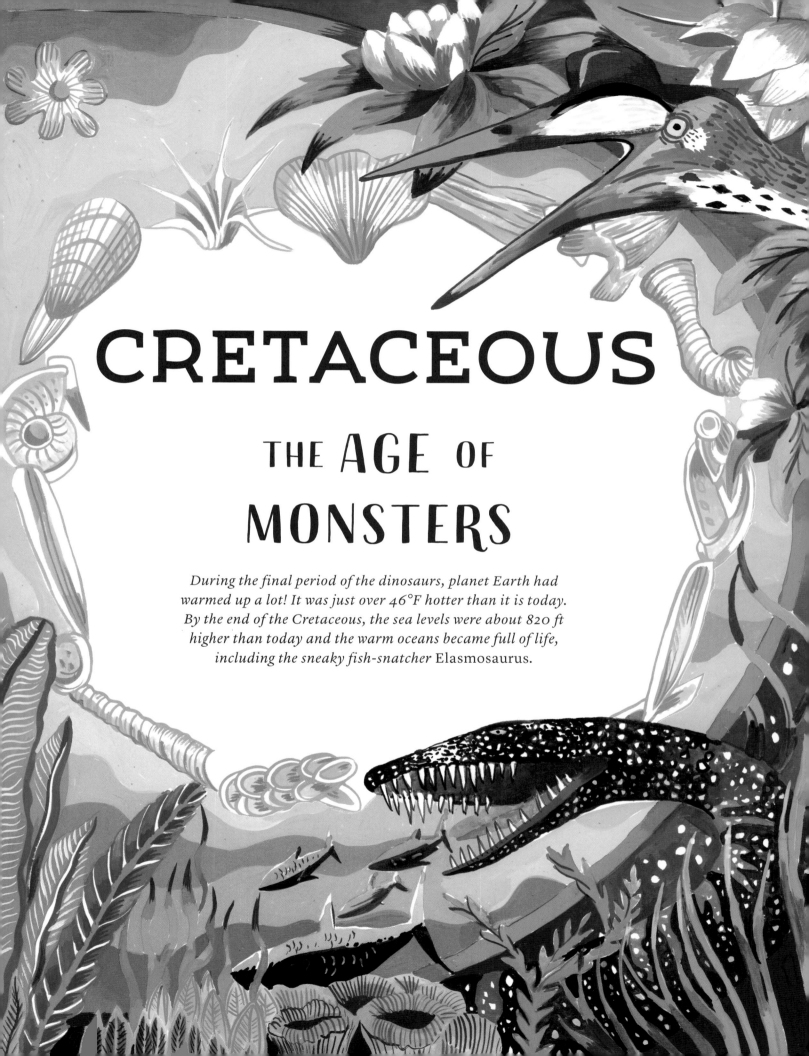

CRETACEOUS

THE AGE OF MONSTERS

During the final period of the dinosaurs, planet Earth had warmed up a lot! It was just over 46°F hotter than it is today. By the end of the Cretaceous, the sea levels were about 820 ft higher than today and the warm oceans became full of life, including the sneaky fish-snatcher Elasmosaurus.

IGUANODON

An early discovery

This big leaf-munching reptile was one of the very first dinosaurs to be examined by scientists. Mary Mantell brought some odd-looking teeth for her husband Gideon, as he was studying the fossils and geology of southern England. He thought that the teeth looked a lot like enormous versions of a lizard's teeth, and so, in 1822, gave the mystery animal a name that means 'iguana tooth'.

The word 'dinosaurs' had not even been invented by this time, and so very little was understood about what *Iguanodon* might have looked like and how it lived. A lot of mistakes were made as the teeth and bones were reassembled in different ways over the years. But today's paleontologists are confident that the bulky *Iguanodon* mainly walked on all fours. Its front limbs were very well developed, with big muscles and sturdy bones, and the bones of the wrist were fused into a large block to help support its weight. *Iguanodon* had a sharp beak at the tip of the jaw that could cut through twigs and leaves, which were then sliced up by the leaf-shaped, jagged back teeth.

One mystery still remains though: the cone-shaped spike found among the bones of some specimens. Early paleontologists thought that these fitted to the nose, like the horns of a rhino. However, later discoveries showed that they were actually large thumb claws that stuck out from the front feet. What were the thumb spikes used for? Did they help *Iguanodon* dig out food, or were they a weapon for jabbing at enemies? Experts are puzzled to this day.

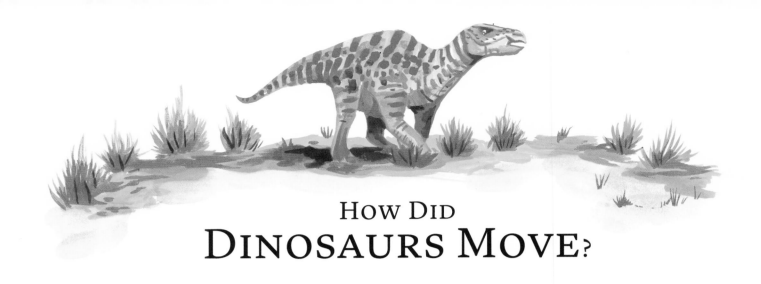

How Did
DINOSAURS MOVE?

People who study dinosaurs and other fossils are called paleontologists. Paleontologists work like detectives, piecing together evidence to find out more about the life of the past. But with only a few clues about what an animal looked like and how it lived, it is easy to jump to conclusions about dinosaurs. Luckily, science is about constantly improving, building on or fixing previous theories to create a more accurate picture.

The way dinosaurs moved is a classic example of this. Dinosaurs were once considered to be slow, lazy reptiles that sprawled around and lounged in swamps to support their weight, but we now know they evolved a range of movement. Their limbs were held directly underneath their body, and their hinge-like ankle bones prevented too much movement of the foot. Bones reveal information about limb lengths and muscle sizes, and fossil footprints show the length of their stride and movement behavior. Some could move quickly and easily, while others needed their limbs to take more weight.

A big step in the study of dinosaur movement was testing ideas using computer models. These models can reconstruct

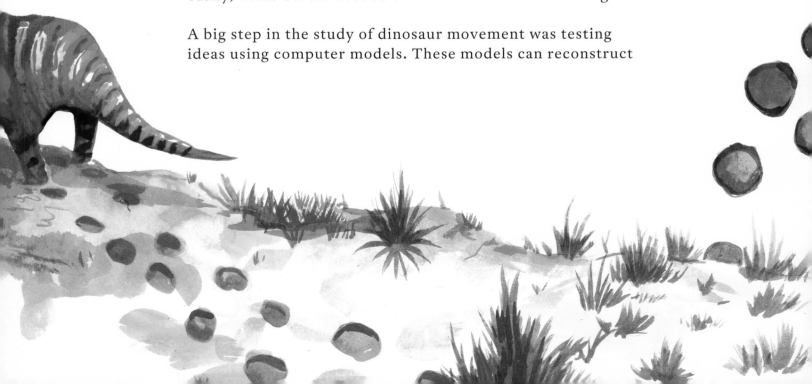

a dinosaur starting with scans of fossil bones and then adding digital muscles, allowing scientists to estimate the forces and strains imposed during movement. Could the bones take the strains of moving quickly? How much force could the muscles exert? Titanic sauropods could not move very fast, for instance: their huge mass meant slow and steady movements were needed to prevent injury. Meanwhile, models of *Tyrannosaurus* show it was too big to run fast, but that it likely used the swing of its tail to make walking more efficient, helping the giant predator save energy during movement.

Much has also been uncovered about the evolution of flight. Theropod dinosaurs took to the air during the Jurassic, joining the pterosaurs and insects as animals capable of powered flight. Feathers evolved into structures that weren't simply useful for keeping warm or showing off, but could take the stress of flying. While computer models have been useful in the study of flight, looking closely at feathers through microscopes has revealed how feathers evolved to help theropod dinosaurs get into the air. Some exceptional fossils preserve the tiny particles that help make up feathers, showing how these changed over time to help increase feather stiffness, eventually allowing birds to explore the skies.

ARGENTINOSAURUS

A titanic herbivore

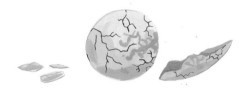

Named after Argentina, where many of its fossils have been found, *Argentinosaurus* was a titanosaur — a giant of giants. The titanosaurs were truly immense, and *Argentinosaurus* is thought to be one of the biggest of them all. But giant sauropods are often known from only a few pieces of the skeleton, and *Argentinosaurus* is no exception. It takes a very long time for such a huge animal to get completely buried, meaning the body is exposed to weather and scavengers for longer, so only a few bones end up being fossilized. Everything we know about *Argentinosaurus* comes from studying just a few bones, such as a thigh bone that is 8.2 ft long and vertebrae that are each as big as a fridge!

From tail-tip to top lip, *Argentinosaurus* is estimated to be almost 115 ft long. With a body weight of 88 tons, as much as 10 African elephants, *Argentinosaurus* was one of the largest animals to ever walk the earth, and walking was all it could do. Such a mighty creature could not run. The forces involved would be too much for the leg bones.

A fully grown *Argentinosaurus* was likely impossible to attack, but babies were easier targets. They hatched from soccer-ball-sized eggs and took several years to reach full size. The adults typically laid their eggs in big breeding colonies like modern-day turtles, so that their young had less chance of being eaten, but the care stopped there. Adults did not look after their young, so if a baby *Argentinosaurus* was to grow into a giant, it had to fend for itself and try not to get eaten!

Caring for Their YOUNG

One of the differences between the first reptile dinosaurs and their amphibian ancestors is their eggs. Amphibians, like frogs and various other early tetrapods, lay soft jellied eggs that dry out very fast. Mostly they are laid in water. Meanwhile, many reptiles have eggs with waterproof shells around the outside, which stop the babies growing inside from drying out. The eggshells do let air through though, so the baby can breathe. That is why these reptiles, and their bird cousins, always lay eggs on land and never underwater.

Given that modern birds and crocodilians lay eggs, it's very likely that their dinosaur cousins did too, and we have plenty of evidence to back this up. In fact, various eggs and nests are known for a range of species. Eggs came in all sorts of shapes, from the rounded eggs of sauropods to the long ones of oviraptorosaurs. However, while many dinosaurs turned into giants, the eggs of these enormous beasts were relatively small. That's because eggs rely on gases passing across the shell to help the developing baby breathe – if the egg was too big, the baby would suffocate.

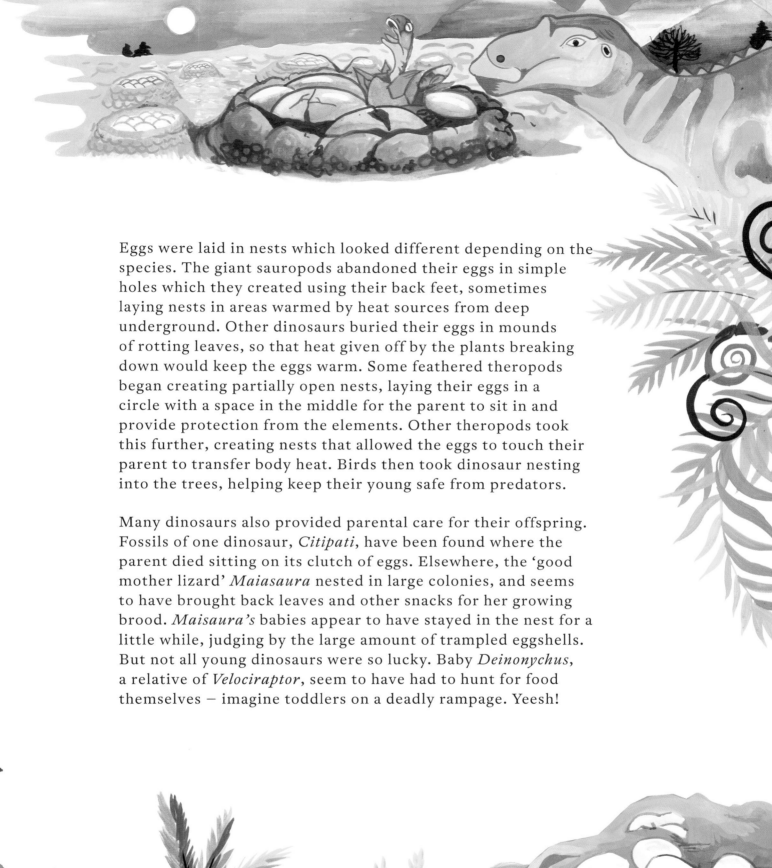

Eggs were laid in nests which looked different depending on the species. The giant sauropods abandoned their eggs in simple holes which they created using their back feet, sometimes laying nests in areas warmed by heat sources from deep underground. Other dinosaurs buried their eggs in mounds of rotting leaves, so that heat given off by the plants breaking down would keep the eggs warm. Some feathered theropods began creating partially open nests, laying their eggs in a circle with a space in the middle for the parent to sit in and provide protection from the elements. Other theropods took this further, creating nests that allowed the eggs to touch their parent to transfer body heat. Birds then took dinosaur nesting into the trees, helping keep their young safe from predators.

Many dinosaurs also provided parental care for their offspring. Fossils of one dinosaur, *Citipati*, have been found where the parent died sitting on its clutch of eggs. Elsewhere, the 'good mother lizard' *Maiasaura* nested in large colonies, and seems to have brought back leaves and other snacks for her growing brood. *Maisaura's* babies appear to have stayed in the nest for a little while, judging by the large amount of trampled eggshells. But not all young dinosaurs were so lucky. Baby *Deinonychus*, a relative of *Velociraptor*, seem to have had to hunt for food themselves – imagine toddlers on a deadly rampage. Yeesh!

QUETZALCOATLUS

The largest flyer ever

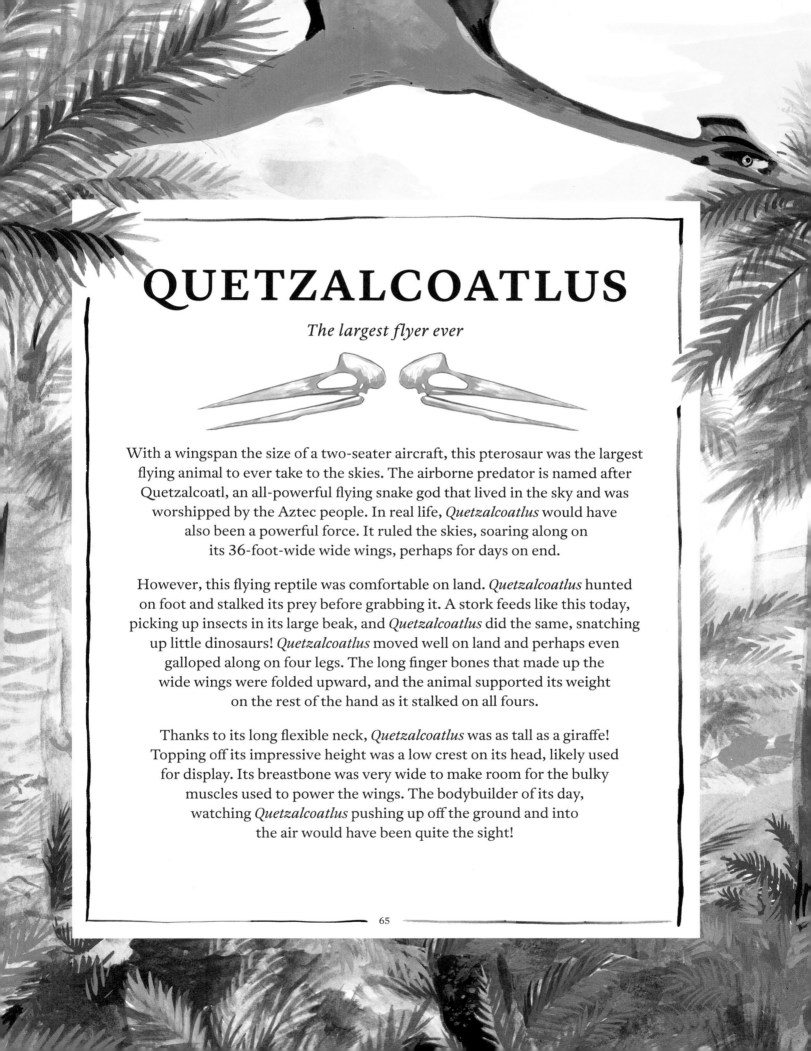

With a wingspan the size of a two-seater aircraft, this pterosaur was the largest flying animal to ever take to the skies. The airborne predator is named after Quetzalcoatl, an all-powerful flying snake god that lived in the sky and was worshipped by the Aztec people. In real life, *Quetzalcoatlus* would have also been a powerful force. It ruled the skies, soaring along on its 36-foot-wide wide wings, perhaps for days on end.

However, this flying reptile was comfortable on land. *Quetzalcoatlus* hunted on foot and stalked its prey before grabbing it. A stork feeds like this today, picking up insects in its large beak, and *Quetzalcoatlus* did the same, snatching up little dinosaurs! *Quetzalcoatlus* moved well on land and perhaps even galloped along on four legs. The long finger bones that made up the wide wings were folded upward, and the animal supported its weight on the rest of the hand as it stalked on all fours.

Thanks to its long flexible neck, *Quetzalcoatlus* was as tall as a giraffe! Topping off its impressive height was a low crest on its head, likely used for display. Its breastbone was very wide to make room for the bulky muscles used to power the wings. The bodybuilder of its day, watching *Quetzalcoatlus* pushing up off the ground and into the air would have been quite the sight!

VELOCIRAPTOR

Fast thief

Velociraptor was a fast-moving, two-legged hunter. It likely also relied on stealth and cunning to corner its prey, too. But a real-life *Velociraptor* was only about the size of a goose and probably looked quite similar to one too, albeit with a long stiffened tail. Birds evolved from cousins of *Velociraptor*, and this little hunting dinosaur was covered from head to knee in feathers.

Velociraptor was a a good predator. Analysis of the brain suggests this hunter tracked moving targets with its eyes, locking on to small, agile prey. *Velociraptor*'s winged arms also show further evidence of the close relationship with birds: the bones of the wrist allowed this little hunter to fold the arm up and protect its long arm feathers, as seen in modern birds. The hands carried short, curved claws that may have subdued its soon-to-be victims, but much of the hunting prowess came from its heavily weaponed feet. The second toe had a long, hooked claw which kept it elevated off the ground. It is likely that the claws were used to pin prey to the ground. *Velociraptor* then leaned down and probably started feeding while its victim was still alive. This is just how eagles catch and kill prey today. If it works, it works!

WHAT KILLED THE DINOSAURS?

About 66 million years ago, every dinosaur except birds disappeared, dying in a mass extinction. The Age of the Dinosaurs was over, but they weren't the only ones affected. Many of the great marine reptiles were wiped out, including the plesiosaurs, as were the ammonites, a group of squid-like creatures that lived in coiled shells. Flying pterosaurs also didn't survive the event. Even some of the eventual survivors took hits, with the extinction affecting fish, lizards and birds too, and around three in four species on Earth disappeared. The mass extinction marked the end of the Cretaceous Period and the start of the Paleogene, but what caused it?

Catastrophe came from outer space. A huge meteorite smashed into what is now a place called Chicxulub on the Caribbean coast of Mexico. The space rock was likely traveling at around 12.5 mi per second (almost 45000 mph) and hit with such force that it left a 110-mile-wide crater which can still be seen today. Life in the immediate vicinity was likely turned to ash in an instant. Dust and bits of rock were launched into the atmosphere, some originating from the meteorite itself as it vaporized on impact. As they rained back